STEP-BY-STEP™
DRAW
FLOWERS
AND PLANTS

MARK BERGIN

BOOK HOUSE
a SALARIYA imprint

This edition first published in MMXIX by
Book House

Distributed by Black Rabbit Books
P.O. Box 3263
Mankato, Minnesota 56002

Cataloging-in-Publication Data is available
from the Library of Congress

Printed in the United States
At Corporate Graphics,
North Mankato, Minnesota

9 8 7 6 5 4 3 2 1

ISBN: 978-1-912233-82-3

CONTENTS

MAKING A START

T he first stage of drawing flowers is to choose your flower and then decide which medium you want to use to depict it. You can draw flowers as found objects in their natural setting or in artificial groupings.

Drawing construction lines to outline petals and leaves will help guide you when drawing flowers, like the ones shown above.

"Artificial" subjects are made when the artist purposely arranges a group of flowers against a backdrop.

'Found' objects are things that catch your eye— such as flowers in a garden setting—and are drawn just as they are.

Sketch simple flower constructions.

Detailed observation of a delphinium.

Saffron crocus in ink.

Practice sketching house plants and flowers around your home.

Sketching everyday objects will help you understand the perspective all around you.

The only way to get better is to keep practicing. If a drawing looks wrong, start again. Keep working at it.

DRAWING MATERIALS

There are many different ways to approach a drawing. Try different materials such as pencils, pen, and ink, brush pens, felt—tip pens, and colored pencils. Each creates a different result that will add variety to your drawings.

Wood anemone silhouette.

Felt—tips come in a range of line widths. The broader tips are good for filling in large areas of flat tone.

Lines drawn in **ink** cannot be erased, so keep ink drawings sketchy and less precise. Don't worry about mistakes as they can be lost in the linework as the drawing develops.

Sketch of foxgloves using a graphic ink pen.

Hard pencils are more gray; soft pencils are blacker. Hard pencils are graded from 6H (the hardest) through 5H, 4H, 3H, 2H, and H.

Soft pencils are graded from B, 2B, 3B, 4B, and 5B up to 6B (the softest).

It can be tricky adding light and shade with an ink pen. Analyze your drawing. The lightest areas should be left untouched. Then apply solid areas of ink to the darkest parts. The midtones are achieved by hatching (single parallel lines) or cross—hatching (criss—crossed lines).

Felt—pen drawing of a common poppy.

WAYS OF LOOKING

There are different ways of drawing a flower composition, from a realistic approach to abstract forms.

Pencil study of a rose.

Try varying the amount of detail in your drawing. The more detailed, the more realistic the result. The more sketchy, the more impressionistic your composition will be.

Floral study in felt—tip pen.

Drawing only the outline of each shape can create a more abstract composition. Look carefully at the spaces between objects— artists call this "negative space."

Working in line with some solid blocks of shading, rather than using a tonal approach, can make your drawing very striking.

Ink-pen study using heavy black tone.

CHOOSING A THEME

The choice of theme is endless and down to individual tastes. It can range from traditional flower arrangements and bouquets to simple garden flowers. Choose whatever inspires you.

Think of a theme you would like to draw and collect the objects you need, or just find suitable flowers in their natural environment.

Colored—pencil sketch of flowers in a container.

Hydrangeas and ribbons drawn in ink.

Roses in a
china vase.

Sketching garden or wild flowers
in their original habitat can add
interest to your drawings.

Making up your own floral
arrangements to sketch gives you
greater control over composition and
lighting conditions.

The sinuous shapes of
bindweed make it an
interesting subject to
sketch. You often find it in
gardens or hedges.

11

COMPOSITION

Composition is the arrangement of the parts of your drawing on the surface of the paper. Even when you're only drawing a single flower, consider whether it will look best in the center of the paper or off center.

The composition of this drawing is based on the golden rectangle. Ever since the ancient Greeks, artists have been fascinated by this graceful proportion.

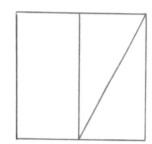

1. Draw a square.

2. Divide it in half. In one half, draw a diagonal.

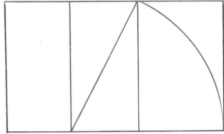

3. Setting your compasses on the ends of the diagonal, draw a curve as shown. This gives the length of your golden rectangle.

A composition based on the golden rectangle. Note how the main flower aligns with the edge of the original square.

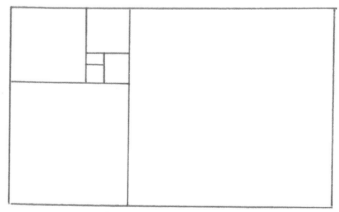

If you remove a square from your golden rectangle, the part left over is also a golden rectangle. You can keep on doing this as many times as you like.

This composition showcases a single plant.

In this composition, simplified flower shapes are carefully arranged to make an all-over pattern.

Subtle differences in the angle of the petals and the curve of the stems add life to this row of nearly identical blooms.

A close-up view of petals can give a completely different impression of a flower.

LIGHT AND TONE

The way light hits an object plays a major role in the outcome of your drawing. It is well worth taking time to consider the direction and strength of your light source.

In this view the light comes from above and casts a shadow below.

Light source

This time the light comes from the front and casts a shadow behind the vase.

Light source

Light source

The light here is coming from the left, so it casts a shadow to the right.

Adding a dark background tone makes the vase and flowers stand out.

A dark background throws the flowers into relief.

NEGATIVE SPACE

Looking at the spaces between the shapes can help you to get the proportions right.

In this ink sketch, dark tones in the foliage make the flowers stand out.

USING PHOTOS

Drawing flowers from photographs can help you to identify shape and form, and will train you to draw accurately.

First choose a good photograph of flowers and trace it. Then draw a grid of squares over the tracing.

Now draw a faint grid of the same proportions onto your drawing paper. Copy the shapes within each square of the tracing paper onto the grid of your drawing paper.

When drawing, remember to keep your viewpoint constant—moving about will change your point of view!

Light source

Once the outline
shape is complete,
add more details to
the drawing. Always
refer back to the
grid for accuracy.

To add form to your
drawing, see where
the light falls, and
add shadows to the
parts that face away
from the light.

Add tone to the
flowers, the background,
and the foreground.

Give the vase a
three-dimensional shape
by using hatching and
cross-hatching.

2-D FLOWERS

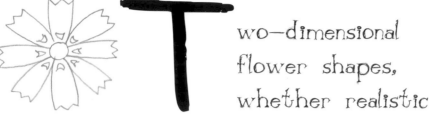

Two—dimensional flower shapes, whether realistic or simplified, really lend themselves to creating interesting designs and patterns.

If an object has a very distinctive shape it may need very little visual information to describe it.

Flattened drawings of flower shapes.

Use your imagination and create your own flower designs using this type of flat drawing technique.

Simple outline drawing of grass and flowers.

Use a dark background to make the flower shapes stand out.

Try filling a whole page with repeating patterns. They don't need to repeat exactly.

Felt pens are useful when drawing two-dimensional flowers because they allow you to block in large areas of flat color quickly.

19

SUNFLOWERS

T
he sunflower is so named because its huge head and fringe of yellow petals are often said to look like the sun.

Begin by drawing three circles, as shown, one inside the other.

Draw in a line for the sunflower stalk.

Try to keep a light touch with these construction lines, as you may wish to erase some of them later.

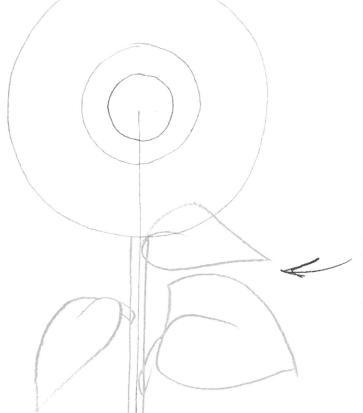

Add another line to thicken the stalk. Draw in big leaves using sweeping pencil strokes.

In the outer ring draw tiny circles to represent the seeds. The seeds in the center are more tightly packed (see detail below).

COMPOSITION

Try framing your drawing with a rectangle or a square—this can make the composition look completely different.

Draw in the petals. Layer them behind each other to create a feeling of depth.

Now begin to add detail to the leaves.

Adding darker shading where the light would not reach will make your drawing more realistic.

Use shading and tone to add the final details to the flower.

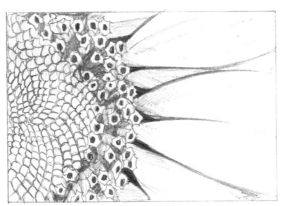

A sunflower head in close—up makes a fascinating study by itself. The tiny flowers in the center (which later become seeds) are arranged in interlocking spirals.

Remove any unwanted construction lines.

ROSES

Roses are widely grown for their beauty and fragrance. Indeed, they are ancient symbols of love and beauty. The rose is the national flower of England.

Draw a large oval with a smaller one inside. Add a line passing through the center for the stem.

The middle of the rose must be drawn with the petals closely clustered together.

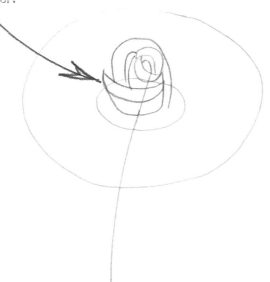

USING A MIRROR

Try looking at your drawing in a mirror. Seeing it in reverse can help you spot mistakes.

Add more petals,
spacing them
farther apart.

Make the stem
thicker and draw
in the leaves.

Sketch in the
outermost petals.

Adding darker shading
to the side that
faces away from the
light will make your
drawing more realistic.

Use shading and tone
to add texture to the
surface of the petals.

Add detail to the
leaves. Give them
jagged edges and veins.

Add thorns to
the stem.

Remove any unwanted
construction lines.

23

DAFFODILS

Daffodils have a unique trumpet—shaped flower and are a cheerful yellow color. The daffodil is the national flower of Wales, where it is traditional to wear one on St. David's Day.

Start by drawing two circles and two ovals, as shown.

Draw the stems, one straight, one bent.

Use these shapes as guides to sketch in the petals.

Add the trumpet shape.

As this flower is viewed from the side, the petals appear narrower because of foreshortening.

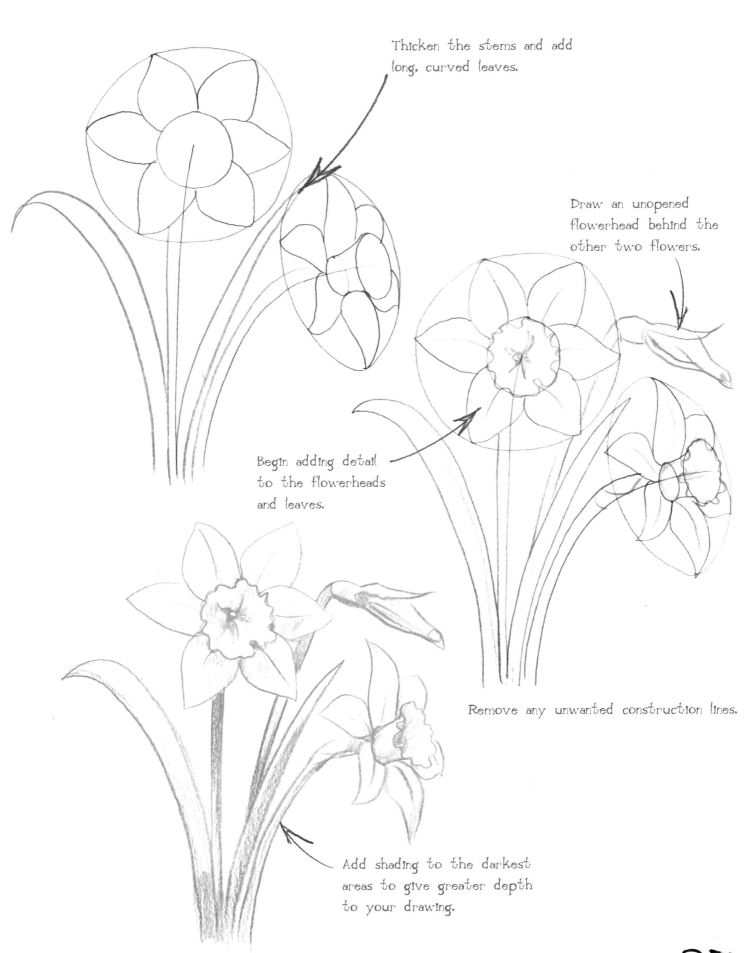

Thicken the stems and add long, curved leaves.

Draw an unopened flowerhead behind the other two flowers.

Begin adding detail to the flowerheads and leaves.

Remove any unwanted construction lines.

Add shading to the darkest areas to give greater depth to your drawing.

25

CHRYSANTHEMUMS

Chrysanthemums come in many colors, shapes, and varieties. The flowerheads are formed from densely packed petals.

Start by drawing two large ovals. Then draw two smaller ovals inside them.

Draw in two lines for the stalks.

Remember to draw these construction lines lightly so they can easily be erased later.

Add a bud shape in between the two large flowerheads.

Add a second line to show the thickness of the stems.

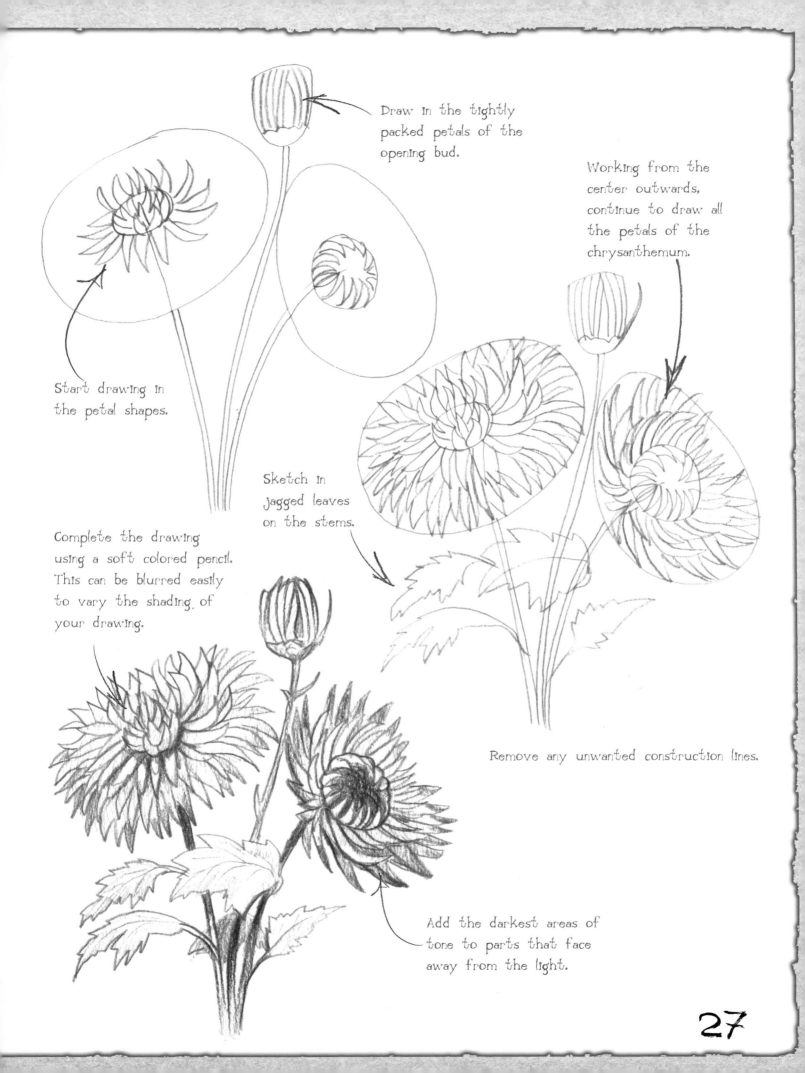

Draw in the tightly packed petals of the opening bud.

Working from the center outwards, continue to draw all the petals of the chrysanthemum.

Start drawing in the petal shapes.

Sketch in jagged leaves on the stems.

Complete the drawing using a soft colored pencil. This can be blurred easily to vary the shading of your drawing.

Remove any unwanted construction lines.

Add the darkest areas of tone to parts that face away from the light.

27

THISTLE

The thistle is the national emblem of Scotland. It is a very prickly flower, but its distinctive shape is rewarding to draw.

Draw ovals for the flowerheads.

Add flowing lines for the flower stems.

Add detail to the lower half of each oval. Then draw in the fan-like outline of the petals on top.

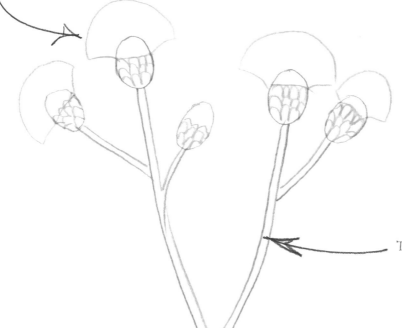

Thicken the stem lines.

28

Add detail to the
flowerheads.

Draw in the leaves.
Use jagged lines to
make them look spiky.

Add veins to the center
line of each leaf.

Complete the final details, adding
shading and toning to give a
three—dimensional effect.

The thistle's head is
densely packed with spikes.
Draw many short lines to
represent these.

Add thorns to the stems.

Remove any unwanted
construction lines.

29

HIBISCUS

Hibiscus plants have large, colorful, trumpet-shaped flowers. These come in many colors, including yellow, pink, red, white, purple, and orange.

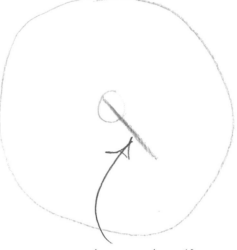

Draw a large circle with a smaller one inside it. Draw a line out from the center.

Keep all construction lines faint so they can be easily erased.

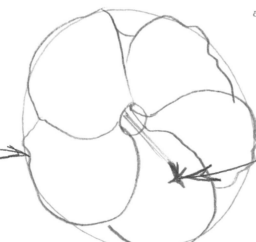

Sketch in five large petals, using your outer circle as a guide.

Add a small star to the end of the line. This will become the stamens.

Start adding details to the petals using small lines.

Add shading to the flower center to create a feeling of depth.

Add little circles to the ends of the stamens.

Draw in some smaller leaves behind the flower.

Begin drawing in the leaves surrounding the flower.

Add veins to the center line of each leaf.

Add shading to the petals, stamens, and leaves. This will give your finished drawing a three-dimensional effect.

This detail of the stamens shows the pollen carried on their ends.

Add the darkest areas of tone where light wouldn't reach.

Remove any unwanted construction lines.

GLOSSARY

Composition   The arrangement of the various parts of a picture on the drawing paper.

Construction lines   Guidelines used in the early stages of a drawing; they are usually erased later.

Cross-hatching   A series of criss-cross lines used to add dense shade to a drawing.

Foreshortening   Drawing part of an object shorter or narrower than it would usually appear, to give the impression that it is angled towards or away from the viewer.

Found composition   A composition in which objects are shown just as the artist found them, rather than being deliberately arranged by the artist.

Hatching   A series of parallel lines used to add shade to a drawing.

Light source   The direction from which the light seems to come in a drawing.

Negative space   The empty space left between the parts of a drawing. It can be an important part of the composition in itself.

Silhouette   A drawing that shows only a solid dark shape, like a shadow.

Stamens   The organs inside a flower that produce pollen.

Three-dimensional (3-D)   Having an effect of depth, so as to look lifelike or real.

INDEX